This Sketch Book Belongs To:

“ Always Keep Sketching
And
Make Things Beautiful ”

Made in the USA
Monee, IL
04 June 2022

97453484R00070